Three Hungry Friends

by **Natasha Gupta**

Illustrations by **Mike Motz**

For little Navya,
who always wants elephant stories

It was a cold December morning in the animal town Pleasantville where Elvis the elephant lived with his parents. He was feeling bored in the house and longed to have a fun outing with his friends.

So he donned his father's brown Fedora hat to keep his head warm and went to call upon his friends, Hector the horse and Cletus the Camel.

Cletus put on a yellow wool scarf, as his neck always got cold, and Hector pulled on a pair of green socks to keep his feet warm and toasty.

They decided to spend the day in the city. Now, the city and animal town Pleasantville were separated by a vast jungle. They all set out for the city happily. They were singing songs, swapping stories, and cracking jokes as they walked.

As the lunch time drew nearer, all three friends began to feel hungry. Elvis's stomach gave a loud growl and scared the other two. They thought it was the sound of some predator lurking nearby. City was still quite far, and the friends were kicking themselves to have forgotten to pack lunch for their journey.

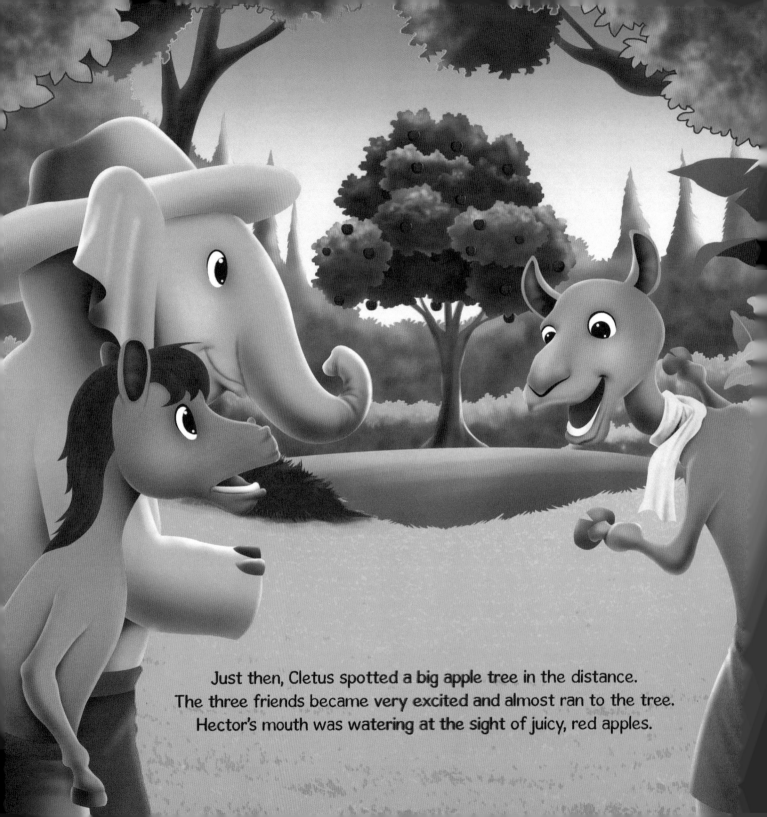

Just then, Cletus spotted a big apple tree in the distance.
The three friends became very excited and almost ran to the tree.
Hector's mouth was watering at the sight of juicy, red apples.

He made a great leap up to the branch carrying
the apples, but just fell short of the branch.
He made a few more attempts, but each time,
he fell slightly short of touching the branch.

Then Cletus said to Hector, "Don't exert yourself, friend! I just need
to raise my neck slightly, and I can get those apples in no time."

So Cletus stretched his neck to the branch, but he too fell just a little short of the apples.
He tried a few times - and even tiptoed on his feet - but could not reach the apples.

Then Elvis reassured them and said, "Don't worry, friends! I will get you a bushel of apples. You should have allowed me to try first since I have such a long trunk. I will pluck those apples and we will soon have a feast under the shade of this tree."

His friends, now tired from all their jumping and stretching, sat down
and waited for Elvis to bring them a bushel of apples. Elvis raised his
trunk as high as he could and swung at the apples on the lowest branch.
But, alas! Even the lowest branch of that tall tree was quite high.
He, too, fell just a little short of the apples.

He swung a few more times at the branch, but to no avail.
Thus, dejected and hungry, three friends sat under the tree
thinking of some other way to get the apples.

Just then, Hector had an idea. "Hey, Why don't we all shake the trunk of this tree, and some apples will fall on the ground for us!"

Elvis and Cletus got excited at the idea and jumped up happily to shake the big tree.

But the apple tree had heard them and he roared with anger.
"You insensitive animals! Do not try to shake me or bump against me.
You are free to have my apples but if you cause me any harm,
it will not be good for you!"

The three friends got scared at hearing apple tree's booming voice.

Elvis apologized to the tree. "We did not mean to hurt you, Mr. Apple Tree.
We are just very hungry. We are not able to reach the apples on your branches.
Do tell us if there is another way to get them."

The Apple tree replied, "There are only two ways to get
these apples. You have to be tall enough to reach the branches like a giraffe
or your parents, or you have to be able to climb the tree like a monkey!"

The three friends once again sat down, too tired and hungry to walk any further. Just then, Elvis spotted a monkey on a faraway tree! He raised his trunk and trumpeted loudly to catch the monkey's attention.

Marshall the monkey came swinging and jumping to the apple tree. The three friends shared their problem with Marshall and begged him to help them in getting some apples.

But Marshall was a very clever and a very greedy monkey. He did not believe in helping others without getting something in return.

So he said to the three friends, "I will gladly help you, but what reward do I get for helping you?"

The three friends were delighted and dismayed at the same time.

Cletus answered, "We do not have anything to offer you at this time, but we can bring you something back from the city."

But Marshall did not like that idea at all. Since he was a very treacherous animal himself, he did not trust others to keep their word either.

So he replied, "I want something right now for these apples or I will not help you."

Then Marshall had a thought. "I know! I will give you three apples each in return for one item of clothing that you currently have."

Hector replied, "What do we have that you want in return for apples?"

So Marshall replied, "Hector, I want your green socks, Cletus's yellow scarf, and Elvis's brown hat!"

At hearing this, three friends got very
annoyed and angry at the monkey.

Elvis said, "Marshall, you are a very greedy monkey! This hat
belongs to my father, and he will be very upset if I give it to you.
Also, we will be very cold for rest of the day without our clothing!"

Hector and Cletus also chimed in. "Yes! You are very mean, Marshall!"

So Marshall replied, "Well! This is my offer to you. If you don't
want the apples, then I will take your leave now!"

But three friends were very hungry and decided to accept Marshall's offer.
They gave him the requested items and got three apples each in return for them.

Marshall was very satisfied with his winnings and
decided to wear these items to show of proudly to his troop.
Meanwhile, the three friends were happily munching away on the juicy apples.

Marshall put on Elvis's brown Fedora hat first, but it was so big for his head
that it slid low over his eyes, and he could not see where he was going!

He stumbled and fell from his branch with a shattering thud on the ground!

The friends looked at him curiously, amused at his fall. He looked ridiculous wearing that giant hat and threw it angrily to the ground. He climbed up the tree again and decided to try Cletus's yellow scarf.

He wrapped the scarf snugly around his neck.
But the scarf was so long that he had to give it many
turns around his neck and yet it was still trailing down!

It was meant for a camel's neck, not a monkey's!

As, Marshall was still struggling, the scarf somehow got looped around the branch and the monkey stumbled and dangled with his scarf from the branch! He got many bruises on his face and arms, and with great difficulty, he pulled himself back on the branch. Disgusted with the long scarf, he untangled himself from it and threw it on the ground.

Marshall still had Hector's green socks and thought to himself, "I still have one item to show to the troop, even if I could not keep the hat and the scarf!" So, he sat on the branch and put on the green socks.

But the socks were so loose for him that they slid down his feet. He again stumbled on his loose socks and came crashing down to the ground!

Marshall had enough by now! He did not care much for the stumbling, dangling, and crashing or for the cuts and bruises on his body. He was so tired and beat up that he could not find the strength to climb up the tree anymore.

The three friends had finished eating their apples and were feeling very much rejuvenated. They had picked up their clothing and were getting ready to continue their journey to the city again.

As Marshall saw them getting ready to leave, he begged to them in a pitiful voice, "Dear friends, please help me climb back to the tree. As you can see, I am very much bruised from the falls."

Elvis replied, "And whose fault is that, Marshall? You could have just given us those apples, but you were being greedy and wanted to take advantage of our situation."

Hector guffawed loudly. "Serves you right, Marshall! You are not our friend!"

Cletus said, "But we are not greedy and unkind! We will help you climb back up the tree. I hope this will be a good lesson for you to remember."

Then Cletus asked Marshall to jump up on Hector. From Hector, he jumped to Elvis, and from Elvis to Cletus.

This helped Marshall to reach very
close to the lowest branch of the tree,
and he could grab the branch.

Marshall apologized to the three friends for his greediness
and thanked them for helping him, despite his behavior. Then he jumped
on a nearby tree and disappeared into the thick forest.

The three friends chortled happily as they went on
their merry way, all the while talking about the sweet apples,
the talking tree, and the greedy monkey!